# REEK

# REEK

ALASTAIR CHISHOLM

ILLUSTRATED BY
GEORGE CALTSOUDAS

union
square
kids
NEW YORK

Union Square Kids
Hachette Book Group
1290 Avenue of the Americas, New York, NY 10104
unionsquareandco.com
@unionsqandco

First published in Great Britain in 2024 by Barrington Stoke Ltd.
First published in the United States and Canada in 2026 by Union Square Kids.

The typeface Barrington Stoke Roman and its fonts are Barrington Stoke's proprietary typeface and font and is used under license from Barrington Stoke.

Union Square Kids is an imprint of Grand Central Publishing, a division of Hachette Book Group, Inc. The Union Square Kids name and logo are registered trademarks of Hachette Book Group, Inc.

Union Square Kids books may be purchased in bulk for business, educational, or promotional use. For information, please contact your local bookseller or the Hachette Book Group Special Markets Department at special.markets@hbgusa.com.

Library of Congress Control Number: 2025938507

ISBN: 978-1-4549-6282-3 (paperback)

Printed in China

Lot#
12/25
LEO
2 4 6 8 10 9 7 5 3 1

Union Square & Co.'s EVERYONE CAN BE A READER books are expertly written, thoughtfully designed with dyslexia-friendly fonts and paper tones, and carefully formatted to meet readers where they are with engaging stories that encourage reading success across a wide range of age and interest levels.

*For Pip and Richard, the smartest grown-ups I know*

# CONTENTS

# 0

# The Reek

When the Reek came, it came *fast*.

That's what surprised everyone. I mean, we'd all heard the warnings about polluting the ground, the seas, the air. We knew we were heading for disaster—we had to fix things *now*, before it was too late! And all the politicians said, "Yeah, yeah, we'll do it tomorrow." Acting like a kid with their homework, you know? Saying, "Tomorrow. We'll fix things tomorrow."

And then something happened.

It was just a smudge at first—a little yellow-brown cloud somewhere over the Pacific. The cloud drifted over the sea. It drifted over a tiny island. No humans there—just thousands of birds.

When the cloud moved away, every bird on the island was dead. And the cloud was bigger.

When the first researchers reached the cloud, it was the size of a town. By the time they escaped, it was as big as a city—a horrible yellow-brown smoke that killed every breathing creature. When it passed over land, everything died. When birds flew through it, they died. The oceans below the cloud couldn't absorb oxygen, and half the fish died. In the first week, the cloud doubled in size. Then again. Then *again*.

How did it happen? Everyone wanted to know. There were theories. Perhaps the cloud was a poison attack, released by some hostile country. Or it was a freak gas eruption from the sea that would disperse—nothing to worry about. It was locusts. It was aliens! (Someone always says aliens.)

We're pretty sure now that it was an experiment gone wrong—someone's clever plan to "fix the planet quick." But whatever it was, Earth was the perfect environment for it—poisoned, polluted, too warm. The scientists called the cloud a "highly self-replicating airborne algal bloom." I don't know what that means.

Everyone else called it the Reek.

It drifted on, as big as a country, then bigger. And finally, *finally* we realized. This was it. This was the disaster we'd all known was coming. It was happening right now.

*We were all going to die.*

Well . . . we didn't. But it was close. An internet billionaire, Axel Brodie, saved us. I mean, he didn't cure the Reek, because no one can. But he worked out how to take the Reeky air, clean it in huge purifier factories, and sell it back to us.

It was a terrible idea. For this to work, we'd be wearing masks and oxygen tanks all the time, *forever*. We'd have to live in bubbles, like we were on the moon or something! It sounded horrific.

But we had no choice.

Zephyr Industries, Brodie's company, saved *billions* of people. We all got used to the masks, and the tanks, and the "Zephyr Air." It was just one more thing we all had to pay for—heating, lighting, food, and now the air we breathe . . .

So, we survived the Reek. And that's what we're doing now. Surviving.

Every day.

Just surviving.

# 1

## Sparrow

*Ping-ping* goes the alarm.

Urgh.

*Ping-ping.*

Ten minutes more—that's all I need. Ten minutes and everything will be fine.

*Ping-ping-ping-ping—*

I groan, stick out a hand, and hit snooze. Then, my eyes still closed, I grope around for my earpiece and put it in my ear.

"Good morning, Sparrow," says Sam's artificial voice.

Sam is my smartpad. Phone, personal computer, digital assistant. I'd be lost without him. Literally lost—he's my map, too. And my alarm clock . . .

But today he's *far* too early. I rub my face. "What's up, Sam?" I mutter.

"New job available," says Sam. "Signed single package, pickup from Duke Street, deliver to Tollcross. Pickup within thirty minutes. Accept yes/no?"

I heave myself up into a sitting position and cough as quietly as I can. Our apartment is supposed to be airtight—our own personal oxygen bubble. But the seals are a bit worn. Some of the Reek manages to seep in overnight, and by morning my lungs always hurt. I reach for my mask and breathe in deeply until the pain eases.

Signed deliveries pay more, so I sigh and say, "Yes. Accept. On my way."

I creep out of bed and get dressed, trying not to wake my little sister, Nina. Grandpa's already up, puttering around the kitchen. He sleeps on the sofa but always puts away his bedding before we get up. He's making a cup of tea and pours one for me.

"Morning, Surep," he says. "Or are you Budgie now?"

I roll my eyes. "Sparrow, Grandpa. I'm Sparrow."

He grins. I still feel a bit sick from the coughing, but the tea helps.

"What are you doing up so early?" Grandpa asks.

I peer outside, where it's still almost dark. It's only six in the morning, urgh.

"Job," I say.

Grandpa sighs. “You were back late last night. You need your sleep, girl.”

We’re low on credit, and it’s only the middle of the month. But I don’t say anything, because it makes Grandpa feel bad. I shrug.

“Nina’s teacher read her story to the class,” Grandpa says. “She says Nina’s got a real talent.” He sounds proud.

We’re both proud of Nina. I was never good at the book stuff, but my little sister’s got a chance to get to high school—maybe even an office job one day. Imagine! In a big place, with a suit and a computer and all the air you can breathe . . . She’d be *rich*.

“You make sure she keeps doing her homework,” I say.

Grandpa smiles. “She will, sweetheart. But what about you?”

“I’m okay,” I reply. “This is a signed package—that’s good money.”

I look around. Our place is tiny. One room for me and Nina, Grandpa in the living room, a

kitchen space with one burner and a tea kettle, and it's freezing even in summer. And we need to fix the seals to stop the Reek getting in. It's not good waking up coughing every day.

*Ping-ping*, whispers Sam in my ear.

"Gotta go," I say.

"You back for dinner?" asks Grandpa. "We've got some real vegetables—*cauliflower*. I'm making a curry."

Real food! "Yum! Don't eat it all without me!" I hug him, and he hugs me back tight. Grandpa's getting a bit thin, but his arms are still strong, and I breathe in his familiar smell as he wraps his arms around me.

"Right," I say. "Come on, Sam, let's go."

I collect my skates and helmet. Then I strap Sam onto my shoulder, and my helmet display flickers on. My flight suit's a bit baggy.

I got it secondhand, or thirdhand, or, I dunno, tenth-hand. I'm pretty small compared to the other couriers—that's why everyone calls me Sparrow. The sleeves wrinkle around my arms, and I fold them up a few times.

I hook up my oxygen tank, fasten my face mask, and give Grandpa a thumbs-up. Then I squeeze into the airlock at our front door. The airlock whines as it sucks the good air back into the apartment, making my ears pop. Then there's a *whoosh* as the outside air comes in, and I step out into the city.

The Reek is thick this morning, and the world is a murky yellow-brown color, like sulfur. Our apartment is high up in a really old, curved tower block, and from our concrete balcony I can see west across Edinburgh. There's the castle, sitting on top of the huge rock in the center. Across from it is another mountain of rock called Arthur's Seat.

Behind the castle, more than twice as tall, is Zephyr Tower, the company headquarters. It looms over everything, owning the city. Lights at the top blink green and red to warn aircraft of its presence. The tower is already half lit up from office workers starting their day. It stands like it's the most important thing in the world.

Well, I mean, it's Zephyr—so, yeah, I guess it is.

I wonder if Axel Brodie is awake at the top of his tower. He has loads of houses, of course, but they say he likes to sleep there so he can keep busy. He never stops.

I strap on my skates. They're not very good, and they cost a fortune. I had to borrow money to pay for them, and the next payment's due in a week. The courier company I work for, Zephyr Deliveries, arranged the loan. The loan company is Zephyr Finance, and *they* link directly to my Zephyr Bank account. Sometimes it feels like all the Zephyr companies are just moving money between each other for fun, and I never see any of it.

I tap my skates together. They activate and gently lift me up until I'm hovering just above the concrete.

"Duke Street?" I ask Sam.

"Correct," says Sam. "You have twelve minutes."

I'd better get going. I unloop my tether, hook it around a nearby pillar . . . and leap off the building.

# 2

## The Job

The wind whips at me as I fall, and I feel that wonderful giddy terror as windows flicker past. Then I haul on the tether and swing back in. I land on another balcony, ten floors down. The skates squeal as they take my weight, sparking against the concrete before cutting out. Useless things. I tap them together and they start working again, lifting me back up.

I flick the tether, and it unhooks and snaps back. My hover skates might not be great, but my tether is the *best*—a super-thin, super-strong cable that rolls back tight enough to fit into my hand. My friend Miriam made it for me, and she's a genius. Smartest grown-up I know, for sure.

I swing down again and reach the ground. I clip the tether to my belt and head to the collection point to pick up my job. Bonzer is there already.

“Titch,” he says to me with a smug grin.

"Bozo," I reply.

Bonzer calls me Titch. He thinks it's funny. Mind you, I always call *him* Bozo, when he says his name is Bonzer. But honestly, who calls themselves *Bonzer*? Bonzer is a name you'd give to a dog.

Bonzer's got half a dozen packages and envelopes. He's a lousy courier, but he's a pal of the desk guy, and he always gets work. Bonzer swaggers past in his big silver boots that he repaints every month. His hair is greasy, but his boots shine.

"Who gave *you* a job, Titch?" Bonzer asks, but I ignore him and go to the counter.

"Collect," I say to Nesbit, the desk guy. Sam sends him the authorization code. Nesbit ignores me.

"Speak up," calls Bonzer. "He can't see you because you're so small." He's so funny.

I wait. One time I rapped on the glass, and Nesbit got annoyed. He gave me no jobs for a week. A *week*. We were gasping on fumes by the end of that. Now I stand patiently until Nesbit looks up.

"Code," he mutters in a bored voice.

*I just sent it to you*, I think, but say nothing. Sam resends it.

Nesbit taps at his keyboard. Finally, the slot by his desk opens and a letter drops out. I collect it, and Sam scans the details.

"Signed delivery," says Nesbit. He doesn't even look at me. "Tollcross, by 6:45 a.m."

Sam pings a warning, and I check the time. "Wait—that's only twenty minutes!" I say.

Nesbit shrugs. "Job changed. You took it."

"But that's not fair!" I complain. "You can't—"

Nesbit gives me a death stare, and I shut my mouth. Am I giving Nesbit grief? I am not. I can't afford to. But I've got twenty minutes to get across town, and rush hour's starting. I stuff the letter into my pack and storm past Bonzer, who's laughing loudly. Outside, I race along the street and kick my skates into life.

“Sam, give me a route!” I shout. You have to make the delivery on time, or you don’t get paid. Worse, you get marked down, and then you get the crummy jobs, so you get marked down *again*, and around and around it goes . . .

“No route to destination in target time,” says Sam in his usual calm voice.

“*Any* route!” I snap.

The traffic is moving pretty well, so there *is* a way . . . I track the cars and trucks going by. *Not this one, not this one* . . . Then comes a white van. *Perfect*. I switch the tether to magnet mode and fling it. Its hook catches on the rear of the van. The cable goes taut, almost pulling my arms out of their sockets. I jam my skates on max power and let the van pull me along. The car behind me toots its horn angrily as I swing in front of it, but I ignore the driver and concentrate on not dying.

The van driver seems to be in a rush, which is good. He races through an orange light. Then through a *red* light . . . Cars honk, and one drives right at me. I leap into the air, land on the hood with a *thump*, have barely a moment to look at the driver's astonished face, and then shoot forward again. On my shoulder, Sam is beeping and pinging warning signals. The van swings round a corner, and I swing out behind it, into the path of a garbage truck.

"ARGH!" I yell.

I haul on the tether and lurch back behind the van, almost toppling over and faceplanting on the road. My skates scrape and spark in fury, and Sam is wailing at me. For a moment I think, *This is it*—

Somehow, I stay upright. The van reaches the top of the hill and turns away. I release the tether from magnet mode, and it snaps back to my hand. I'm halfway there, and I only half-died—result!

"Time, Sam!" I say.

"Twelve minutes."

I speed up. Edinburgh is a city of hills, built on layers and layers of streets and houses.

I leap down to the lane fifteen feet below, hooking the tether over the iron railings to break my fall.  Now I head west, under the shadow of the castle.  I look for another handy van to help me up the next hill, but there's nothing, so I'm panting by the time I climb the steps to the delivery point and jab the intercom button.

"Time!" I gasp to Sam.

"Three minutes."

I lean on the button until I hear a grumpy voice.  "For goodness' sake, what do you want?"

"Delivery!" I reply.

The intercom tuts.  "Just put it through the slot!"

"Gotta sign," I say.

The intercom tuts again.  There's a *really* long wait, and then a woman stomps up and glares at me through the glass door. I wave the letter.

"Sign, please," I say, holding Sam up.

The woman peers at the letter. She peers at Sam's screen. She peers again at the letter. Finally, she scowls and leans toward the glass so Sam can scan her face.

"Confirmed," he says, and I shove the letter into the slot.

"Delivered!" I snap.

Sam beeps. "Confirmed. Delivery complete. Time: 6:44 a.m."

I slump against the door. Delivered on time. Paid. Might even cover the oxygen I just used up . . .

"New job available," says Sam. "Pickup at Conference Center, deliver to George Street. Accept yes/no?"

There's a rapping on the glass door. I look up to see the woman flicking her hand at me to tell me to go away. I want to flick her my own hand signal, but I can't afford a bad review.

"Yes. Accept," I groan to Sam.

I stagger down the steps and head up into town. And so begins another beautiful day.

# 3

## Axel Brodie

I grab a sandwich at the Base between jobs.

The Base is a cafe. It's not good, but it's cheap and fast and they have clean air, so I can remove my mask for a few minutes. I unclip it and collapse onto a seat.

"How we doing, Sam?" I ask.

"Six deliveries, total charge: twenty-nine credits," says Sam. "Tank status: 12 percent remaining."

I might make forty credits today. But refilling my tank at the Zephyr Air machine will mean ten credits gone right away. Ten more for the air at home, ten for food shopping, six to go toward Nina's new school uniform, two for this terrible sandwich . . .

Two credits remaining. I spend one on a hot chocolate and wrap my freezing hands around it. I watch the news on my table screen and link my headset to the audio.

". . . here at Edinburgh Zoo," it's saying, "where Zephyr CTO Axel Brodie officially opened the new Preservation Dome." And there he is, Axel Brodie, smiling as he cuts a ribbon. The Preservation Dome is a sealed space for the animals that survived the Reek. There aren't many. We lost the giraffes, the tigers, the polar bears, the penguins . . .

Brodie does an interview. He's about fifty and looks nice in a nerdy kind of way. He has glasses, and he must like them because he could easily afford contacts or even new eyes, probably. He's Axel Brodie, after all. He's the World's Smartest Man. He's richer than God.

“We have to preserve whatever we can,” Axel’s saying, looking at the camera with the serious expression he often has. “We’ve lost so much, but this is a first step to normality. Yes, life is different now. It’s been fifteen years since the Reek was detected, and we’re still making sacrifices. But we won’t give up.”

I dunno. Zoos? No one I know can afford to go to one. And I don’t see the rich folks doing much sacrificing. But now Axel’s talking about research. Apparently, some fools are still working without a license, researching the Reek illegally—even running new experiments on the atmosphere.

“I’m sorry, but it makes me angry,” Axel says. “We know the Reek, and all its devastation, came from uncontrolled experimentation. And yet some people are *still* determined to put us all at risk with these dangerous contraptions! For what—personal gain? Fame? Who knows what damage they could do? Zephyr Systems is working twenty-four hours, seven days a week, to purify the air you and I breathe. We've invested huge resources into reducing the Reek. If it could be done, *we would do it*. The people trying their own experiments are playing with death for all of us."

Axel stops, adjusts his glasses, and gives a lopsided smile. "Sorry," he says. "You got me going."

The interviewer apologizes, too, and they go back to talking about wombats, or dodos, or elephants, or some other extinct animal. I wonder who Axel was talking about. I can't imagine anyone so reckless they'd take such a risk . . .

Sam beeps at me with a schedule for this afternoon. Three more jobs. I accept, lick the crumbs of my sandwich, drag my mask back on, and head out.

The jobs go fine. It's raining—big heavy rain where each drop is like a water balloon. It keeps most folks off the streets, so I don't have to fight my way past them. I finish about eight, getting some bonus credits from a last-minute job. It's dark and cold. My skates are heavy and running low on charge, sparking as they scrape the ground.

I reach our tower block and trudge up the concrete stairs, exhausted. The lights are out and I step carefully, but as I reach our floor, I clatter into someone.

"Ow!" I shout.

I trip right over them, slapping to the floor and cracking my elbow on the concrete. I curse. Is it a mugger? It's been years since the police came around here. These days that's all handled by Zephyr Security—ZedSec—and they mostly hang around the rich parts of town. This is a rough area, and my skates, the tether, and Sam are worth stealing. But my attacker gives a yelp, and right away I know it's not some thief. I recognize that yelp.

"For God's sake," I snap. "Why are *you* here?" I flick on Sam's flashlight and see Jamie Souness sprawled out before me. His white face is pinched with pain, and he's holding his knee. I guess I kicked him as I went down.

Good.

I've known Jamie forever. We played together at school, were joined at the hip. He's big and shy; I'm small and sassy. He has pale skin; mine's dark. He has big, wide blue eyes that look surprised all the time; mine are brown, and every photo of me looks like I'm scowling. But we used to be friends.

"Hey, Surep," Jamie says in his soft voice.

"It's Sparrow," I say. "Go away."

Jamie clambers to his feet. "You could say hello, you know," he says. "You don't have to be rude."

"*You* don't have to be hanging around in the dark waiting to jump on folks, but here you are, huh?"

Jamie looks at me. Doesn't say anything, just puts on those sad puppy eyes like he doesn't understand why everything's changed. But of course it has. Because all the time I thought we were friends, Jamie's parents were giving him extra books and tutoring him so he'd pass his tests and get into high school.

Now I'm working while Jamie sits in a classroom with all the air he needs. I'm chasing vans while he's reading books. And when Jamie leaves school, it'll be a nice job for him, and he'll never even remember me. I'll be here, stuck here forever, working for lousy air credits just to stay alive—

"Are you okay?" Jamie asks, and I blink.

"Get lost," I say.

"I was just dropping something off—"

"Get *away*," I interrupt him. "Go back to your nice little house." I turn away and leave him in the dark. After a few seconds, I hear him limp down the steps.

At the apartment, I climb into the airlock and wait as it ejects the Reeky air. It gets stuck sometimes, and I have to give it a kick before it will let me in, but finally I'm home. I pull off my mask and breathe in the warm rich smells of garlic and curry paste. Grandpa is at the stove stirring a pot. Nina is sitting at the table playing on her tablet.

"Surep!" Nina says. "Look, I got a high score!"

I come over and hug her, and she shows me the screen.

"Very good," I say. "How's your homework?"

"Done," says Grandpa.

I study Nina. "Done?" I ask. "Or kind of done?"

Nina hesitates, and I nod.

"Screen away," I tell her. "Finish it properly."

"Give her a break, sweetheart," says Grandpa, but I won't.

"Nina, you need to pass your tests," I say. "You don't want to end up like me—understand?"

I remember Jamie's white face in the darkness and find myself getting angry again, gripping her arm. "You need to pass."

“Ow!” snaps Nina, pulling away. “You’re always horrible to me! We were having fun!”

“Nina—” I say.

She storms out and slams the door. Grandpa says softly, “She’s doing her best, sweetheart.”

“She needs to do more,” I tell him. “She has to pass.”

Grandpa nods. “Well, this could help.” He shows me a secondhand school tablet. Old, but good quality.

“Where’d you get this?” I ask.

“Your friend James just came around with it,” Grandpa says. “He was asking about you.”

I say nothing.

Grandpa serves up three bowls. “Go be nice to your sister and tell her dinner’s ready.”

# 4

## Miriam Fenn

Tuesday, I get a break between jobs and go visit Miriam.

Miriam lives near the docks, in an old junkyard with a faded blue sign that reads "Archibald and Sons, 1929." There are piles of wrecked cars, washing machines, and bathtubs lying rusting. Behind them is the warehouse where Miriam works—works, sleeps, never leaves. Miriam is weird. I really like her.

She's at her workbench when I enter, peering at something through a giant magnifying glass. She's wearing goggles and holding a small welding torch that fizzes bright in the gloomy warehouse. Behind Miriam is a tiny camper and more piles of stuff. Tablets, alarm systems, server, drones . . . I'm amazed no one robs her.

Miriam shuts down her welding torch and stands up straight. “Morning, Sparrow.”

“Morning, Mir,” I say, and glide in on my skates. They’re making a whining noise. I think they’re on their way out, and I haven’t even finished paying for them.

Miriam lifts her goggles. Miriam’s as old as Grandpa and wrapped in a tatty brown shawl. Her hair is a mass of wiry ropes, but her face is young and always curious, and her eyes glint.

“What’s up with your skates?” Miriam asks.

I scowl. “They’re trash.”

Miriam purses her lips. “It’s the 350 series. Flashy looks, trashy quality. They’re losing hover, I bet. Really, you need the 7 series for proper work.”

“Oh, yeah, I’ll go pick up a pair,” I say. “They’re only about ten thousand credits, right?”

Miriam grins. “Want me to upgrade them?” she asks. “I’ve got some motors I’ve been experimenting with, somewhere . . .”

“Really?” I say.

“Sure.” Miriam rubs her finger and thumb together. “But what’s in it for me?”

I glare at her for a second. Then I bring out a plastic tub from behind my back.

“Gobi masala,” I say. “And a naan. And *three* bhajis.”

Miriam laughs. “It’s a deal!”

Her camper has its own airlock system that I think she built herself out of plastic sheets and Plexiglas. It looks rickety, but it seems to work. Inside, we take off our masks, and Miriam zaps the curry in the microwave. Then she dives in as if she hasn’t eaten for two days. She probably forgot.

“How’s the tether?” Miriam asks, licking grease and motor oil off her fingers.

“Brilliant!” I tell her about my chase across town for the signed delivery, swinging from the back of the van. Most adults at this point would wail about safety, but Miriam just wants to know how fast I was going and how sharp the corners were so she can calculate the magnet’s strength.

Miriam’s a genius. She’s always tinkering with something, inventing something, or blowing something up. She’s completely cool and never talks to me like I’m a kid. Which I guess I’m not, because I have a job and I’m looking after everyone. But still, most adults act like I know nothing. Miriam never does. She’s got family, like her nephew, Lil’ Billy, who lives nearby. She talks about him a lot. But she lives by herself and almost never goes out.

“There he is again!” Miriam shouts suddenly, and I jump. She’s glaring at the screen, which is showing a repeat of Axel Brodie at the zoo. Axel’s looking brave and sad and talking about “preserving what we can.”

“Why doesn’t he actually do something about it?” Miriam demands.

Miriam always gets angry at Axel Brodie, which is a bit weird. I mean, lots of folks don’t like his companies. Zephyr owns everything and pretty much everyone. But Axel . . .

“It’s not his fault,” I say. “He didn’t make the Reek.”

“But he could fix it, couldn’t he?” Miriam snaps.

I frown. “I dunno. I mean, he kind of did, right?”

Everyone knows *that*. Axel Brodie was a billionaire, and Zephyr was already big when the Reek hit. He turned all his companies, and all his money and energy, into saving the world, like everyone else—but where they failed, he succeeded. He found a way to purify the Reek from the air.

"We're alive because of him," I say.

"Is this living?" demands Miriam. "Scraping by, working all hours for his rotten company just to breathe? We're servants now." She angrily chews a piece of naan. "Anyway, the man owned a research lab—he didn't do the work himself, did he?"

"No, Mir," I say meekly.

Miriam nods triumphantly. "Exactly! Probably one of his lackeys, huh?"

"Yes, Mir."

She glares at me. "You're mocking me," she mutters.

"Yes, Mir," I say, grinning.

"You're a wretched child. No respect," Miriam grumbles. After a moment, she says quietly, "I knew Axel, once."

She's said this before, but it still gives me a thrill. It's like knowing someone who once shook hands with God. If Miriam boasted about it, I'd understand, but she always acts like it's a sad thing.

"Zephyr wasn't like this before," she says. "Axel really was trying to save us. But these days . . . Do you think he even *knows* what the real world is like? Real people? He's surrounded by press teams, bodyguards, marketing execs . . ." She shakes her head. "I sometimes think, if we could just *show* him . . ."

Miriam wipes her hands on her shawl and stuffs the last bhaji into a pocket for later.

"Well," she says, "tell your grandpa thanks. That meal was nearly as good as your old nana's!"

Back in the warehouse, Miriam roots through some equipment and drags out a pair of old hover skates.

"You can use these till I get yours fixed," she says.

She tosses them to me, and I stagger a bit. They're about twice as heavy as mine. But they're powerful, and when I start them up, they take my weight, no problem. I hover just above the warehouse floor.

"Cool, thanks!" I say.

"Give me two days to fix your old ones." Miriam gives me a strange smile. "Might have something else for you, too."

"Yeah, what? A new tether?"

"No, something else." Miriam chuckles. "The tether's for holding on to stuff. *This* is for breaking free . . ."

I wait, but she doesn't say anything else, so I wave and head off. Miriam has already turned back to her work.

It takes a couple of minutes to get used to the new skates. Between that and checking my jobs, I'm only half paying attention. But as I head around the corner, something catches my eye. I look back to see two men standing in a doorway on the other side of the road.

One man is huge, like a slab of muscle. His neck's as wide as his head, which is shaved. He's wearing a T-shirt despite the cold, standing with his vast arms crossed. The one next to him is thin, and his leather jacket droops around his shoulders. His face droops, too, and so does his lank hair. His hands are in his pockets.

The big man is watching Miriam's warehouse.

The thin man is watching me.

# 5

## Upgrades

Wednesday and Thursday go past in a blur. It's wet—that steady, endless Edinburgh rain that seems to come from nowhere and hangs in the air. But at least it keeps the pedestrians inside, out of my way. Miriam's skates are heavy but reliable, and I zip across the city for twelve, thirteen hours each day.

Nina's birthday is coming up. She's growing out of my old school clothes, too—she's going to be tall, like Nana was. That's another cost. Grandpa's pension barely covers the rent, and these days he's too unsteady to work. He feels guilty, but it's not his fault, is it?

There's only me to look after everyone. Every night I stagger back to the apartment, and Grandpa puts out a plate of soup that I'm too tired to eat. Every night I unclip Sam and count the credits in and out. Some days my jobs barely pay for the air I use. Some mornings I can hardly drag myself out of bed. I run down my oxygen tank until I'm gasping, trying not to waste a single breath. I know Grandpa's doing the same, wheezing away and waving a hand to pretend he's fine.

I get up. I work my deliveries. I count our credits, trying to work out how to pay for food and drink and air this week. I fall into bed. Around me are thousands of people all doing the same—trying to get by.

We're not trying for a better tomorrow . . .

We're just trying to survive today.

I don't make it back to Miriam's until Saturday evening. As I reach her junkyard, I glance around, but I don't see the two men. I wonder if I should tell Miriam about them, but I know she'll just tell me I'm worrying too much. Inside, Miriam is working at her bench as always, and the overhead lights are off. In the half-dark, the welding torch spits and flares, leaving bright red lines of afterglow across my vision.

Miriam stops and lifts her goggles, beaming. "Good timing!" she says. "Nearly finished here. Put the tea on. I'll be right with you."

I head into her little camper and switch on the kettle. I begin pouring out the tea—black for me, white with four sugars for Miriam. She bustles in, carrying something under a tarp.

Miriam drags off her oxygen mask. Underneath, her skin is marked with red lines, and she has bags under her eyes. She seems exhausted, but there's a kind of gleeful look on her face, too. She takes a huge swig of the tea.

"Ooh, lovely, thank you," she says. "How's things?"

I shrug. "Same old. You?"

"Been busy." Miriam pats the tarp. Then she clicks her fingers. "Got your skates—hang on."

She roots around in a cupboard, dragging out piles of half-mended, half-invented gadgets. "Nope. Nope. Nope—oh, yeah, I have to fix you—nope, nope . . ."

While Miriam's back is turned, I try to peek under the tarp, but she suddenly swings around, holding my old hover skates and beaming.

"Bingo!" she says. "Here you are."

I inspect them. They don't look very different, but the bases are a bit thicker.

"I've fixed the motor," Miriam says. "And given them a bit of a boost. Careful when you try them out."

"Fantastic. Thanks, Mir!" I reply.

Miriam shrugs. "Don't mention it. I've got a patch for Sam, too. Hang on." She lifts her pad and holds it against Sam.

"Upgrades acquired," says Sam. "Restarting . . ."

Miriam nods her approval. "Should give you a bit of a boost when you're bidding for jobs," she tells me. "And I added some shortcuts about town. And . . . one or two other things."

I raise an eyebrow, but she doesn't explain.

"Got something else," Miriam says, and unwraps the tarp. It's an oxygen tank, a bit like mine, about the size of a big water bottle. It's gray and chipped but seems sturdy.

"Oh, nice! Where'd you get this?" I ask. Tanks are expensive. I can only afford one, and it's a pain, needing to stop and refill it when you're on a job. Having a spare would be handy.

Miriam waves a hand. “Dug it out of a pile of stuff. I’ve tested it, and it’s sound. Give it a try.”

I connect the tank and activate it. It beeps quietly and shows its reading: 100 percent. “Aw, you filled it,” I say. “Thanks!”

Miriam shrugs.

I pull my mask on, feel the gentle push of air, and take a breath.

“Seems to work,” I say.

Miriam is gazing at me as if expecting something else.

“Thanks!” I say again, and she nods.

“No problem.” Miriam stands up abruptly. “Well, want to try out your skates?”

I put them on outside the camper and kick-start them into life. The skates hum and lift just off the ground with no effort at all. Miriam grunts with satisfaction.

"Take a test drive," she says, "and then I'll finish tuning them." She adds, a little too casually, "Test out the new tank, too."

I peer at Miriam, but her face gives nothing away, so I head out from the warehouse into the dusky city. It's almost dark now, but warm and still. I can hear the hiss of air from my tank and some sort of soft ticking sound. The skates are as smooth as glass, better than ever, and I grin. I tap Sam.

"Hey, Sam," I ask. "How's things?"

Sam gives a little chirrup. "All systems good."

I roll my shoulders forward, feeling the weight of the new tank. "All right," I say, grinning. "Let's have a bit of *fun*."

# 6

# Improvements

The new skates are *amazing*!

I do a couple of test runs across the junk piles, zipping between wrecked cars and swooping over rusted washing machines. The skates' motors hum beneath my feet with quiet power.

I leave the yard and skate past old warehouses and the former police station with its sooty black pillars, then head toward the city center. I skip across intersections, ignoring the angry honking of drivers. I leap onto their hoods and away before they can react. I fling my tether around a lamppost and heave myself into a 90-degree turn down a side street.

Miriam Fenn is a stone-cold *genius.*

Sam flicks up street patterns and traffic warnings onto my helmet display. He seems faster, too—more of Miriam's clever tricks, perhaps? He chirrups and whispers to me like we're the only living creatures in the world. My mask hisses gently, and the new tank seems good. As I reach the city center, I check my oxygen levels.

100 percent.

I stop and check again. 100 percent. I've been out for thirty minutes, breathing heavily—I should be down to 90 percent or less. The tank's not reporting right. But if that's true . . . perhaps it wasn't full when I set out. Heck, it might be nearly empty!

I switch tanks and check my old one: 83 percent. Plenty. I unfasten the new tank and give it a shake. Hmm. As I'm heading back along the main street, I call Miriam.

“Sparrow!” she says, her face ghost-like on my display. “How are you getting on?”

“The skates are *awesome*, Mir!” I say. “What did you do?”

Miriam grins. “Replaced the motor with something I designed myself. Fixed your dampeners, tightened the suspension. And I disabled most of the safety controls. If you stress them too much, I suppose they might catch fire.” She scratches her cheek. “Probably should have mentioned that.”

“Ye-ah,” I say slowly. “Probably . . .”

Genius. But also, I remind myself, totally and completely bonkers.

“Anyway,” I say, “the skates are great, but your tank is flaky. Keeps showing full.”

Miriam nods. “But it works, yes?”

“I guess, but how will I know if it’s running out?”

“And the air’s good?” Miriam asks.

I shake my head, puzzled. “Well, yeah. It’s just air, Mir.”

Miriam leans back and smirks. “The reading’s fine, Sparrow. The tank’s working perfectly.”

“But how can it still be on 100 percent? It must have gone down a *bit*, Mir—it’s not just making air out of nothing . . .”

I stop.

I stare at the tank. It looks ordinary—a battered gray canister with a worn Zephyr logo. Only, I realize now that the base is wrong. The bottom isn’t sealed, and inside I can make out a ring of thin metal fins.

I cover the base with my hand. The tank beeps and its reading goes red. I lift my hand and the reading turns green. I hold my hand just over it and I can feel air being pulled into the tank, just faintly.

"Mir," I say slowly. "What is this?"

"What do you think?"

Stone-cold genius. Totally and completely bonkers.

"You tampered with a tank!" I shout. Then I look around, terrified someone might have heard me. Oh, no. Oh, *no*.

Miriam tuts. "Relax, Sparrow, it's only a little adjustment—"

"But the Reek!" I almost screech.

It's the one rule everyone knows. Zephyr purifies the air, Zephyr makes the tanks—and no one is *ever, ever* allowed to mess with them.

Messing with the environment is what caused the Reek!

"Sparrow, it's fine—" Mir starts to say.

"And the tanks are tamper-proof anyway!" I shout. I want to throw it away, but I don't even know what will happen if it hits the ground. Maybe it will explode! "They'll know you've hacked it. Mir, you'll go to jail for this! *I* could go to jail!"

"*Sparrow!*" snaps Miriam. "Calm down and listen!"

I glare at her image on my display as she gives a long, frustrated sigh. "First, I could disable Zephyr tamper locks before you were even born, Sparrow. It's not exactly rocket science—and I actually *was* a rocket scientist, by the way. And second, tinkering with an old oxygen tank won't cause Armageddon or a new Reek or whatever they tell you—that's nonsense."

She nods and continues, "Look, I should have told you. I'm sorry. But you had your other tank, and I needed you to see for yourself. Head back and I'll explain. Trust me—this is going to change *everything.*"

Miriam hangs up, and I fume. I can't believe she did this! But I must admit, I'm curious, too. I mean, you hear stories. Someone claims they've come up with a gadget to fix the Reek, and they're a celebrity for twenty minutes. But something always goes wrong—it's a fake, or it self-destructs, or catches fire. Or it's a fake that self-destructs and *then* catches fire.

Axel Brodie is the only person to discover how to purify the Reek safely, and Zephyr has the only working purifiers in the world. Even Miriam couldn't have figured it out . . . Could she?

I coast back toward her yard, holding the new tank. I don't know what to do with it. I could go to prison just for *knowing* about it. I stuff it inside my backpack, out of sight.

The Reek is thick this evening, its yellow-brown tendrils of pollution filling the streets, and something is burning. The atmosphere is a soup of smoke and poison. I was sucking air on that tank for thirty minutes. It was good air.

Could it be true?

Sam beeps at me. "Danger ahead," he murmurs. "Fire services active."

A map appears on my display. I stare at it. "Miriam?"

Without thinking, I kick my skates into high gear and charge through the back streets. My heart races as I reach the corner and around—

I stop, panting.

"MIRIAM!" I yell.

Miriam's warehouse and the whole yard are on fire.

# 7

## Fire

"Mir!"

The warehouse roof is on fire, long orange flames leaping into the night. The heat is incredible. The junkyard is burning as well, all the wiring sparking blue, and the air feels dirty. A small crowd has gathered, and I push past them, race to the door, and heave myself at it.

"Ow!"

The handle burns my hand. *Think, Sparrow!* I drag my sleeve down and try again, and the door opens. Black smoke pours out.

"Miriam!" I look back, but no one else is helping—they're just staring at the fire, pointing as old toasters explode in the heat. “Sam, can you detect Miriam?”

“Negative,” Sam replies.

I growl. There’s no choice. I check the seal on my mask and force my way through the smoke inside.

It’s dark. The heat squeezes me like a fist and piles of equipment are burning, but Miriam’s corner is still untouched by the blaze.

“Warning,” says Sam. “Abnormal temperature may invalidate my warranty.”

“You and me both,” I mutter.

Miriam’s bench is deserted, but I check the camper. There she is, lying half out of the airlock, not moving. One hand is clutching an envelope. There’s blood on her head and she’s pale, but at least her mask is on.

“Mir, wake up!” I shout. Nothing. I get my hands under her armpits and *heave*.

Miriam’s a big woman, and I’m a sparrow. I drag her about six inches before collapsing. “Wake *up*, Mir!” I slap her face.

She groans.

“Come *on*!” I scream.

Miriam takes a long shuddering breath and opens her eyes, then looks around, shocked. I help her to her feet. The smoke’s thicker now. We stumble away, but Miriam stops.

“Wait!” she says. She totters back and grabs the envelope. Then, together, we stagger out into the night air.

My eyes are streaming as we collapse to the ground. I’m worried about the blood on Miriam’s head.

“Are you okay?” I ask, panting. “What happened?” *How did the fire start? Was it her welding torch? Was it her experiments with the tank?* My stomach lurches. *Oh, Mir, what have you done?*

“Outside,” she mutters.

“What?”

Miriam coughs and tries again. “Started . . . outside.” Suddenly, she reaches up and grabs me. “You have to get this to him.”

“What? Who?” I ask.

“Axel,” she says, and shoves the envelope at me. “You have to deliver this to Axel Brodie!”

I gape at her. “Miriam, you’re not well,” I manage. “You need a hospital—”

“*LISTEN TO ME!*”

Her voice is fierce. She drags me toward her and hisses in my ear, “I’m sorry. I thought there’d be more time. But I have a job for you.”

And she tells me the plan.

I can’t tell if she’s delusional. But Miriam doesn’t *sound* delusional. At the end, she makes me hold up Sam, and she presents her face to his screen to confirm the order.

Sam pings and says to me, “New job available. Client specifies delivery agent Surep McNab to deliver one packet to Axel Brodie at Zephyr Tower, personal receipt required. Accept yes/no?”

My mind is reeling. Axel Brodie owns the *world*. You can’t just book a delivery to his home! This is crazy!

“Accept yes/no?” Sam asks me again. Miriam watches me.

“Yes. Accept,” I say at last.

Miriam sags. “Jamie can help,” she murmurs. Then her eyes flutter, and she falls back.

“Miriam!” I shout.

Suddenly, there are others around us. Fire officers rush past with hoses. Two paramedics, women in green uniforms, lift Miriam onto a stretcher and carry her to an ambulance. I stumble after them, but one of the paramedics stops me.

"You were inside?" she asks. "How's your breathing? Did your mask seal break?"

I shake my head. "I'm okay."

The paramedic makes me hold out my arms, checks me over, and nods. "We're taking her to the emergency room. If you become dizzy or have problems breathing, see your doctor—understand?"

I nod. As if I have time to see a doctor. As if I could *afford* to see a doctor.

The paramedic gives me a bottle of water. "Well done, kid," she says. "You probably saved her life."

The ambulance leaves. I stand around, a bit dazed. The blaze is under control—or maybe there's not much left to burn. Miriam said the fire started outside. Did someone start it on purpose? Who would do that?

With horror, I remember the two men from a few days ago. I should have told Miriam about them! They're not here now, but they *were* watching her, weren't they? And Miriam just gave me a delivery order direct to Alex Brodie's apartment. That's not allowed—how did she do that? And the air tank . . .

"You!" shouts someone. I turn and see two Zephyr Security officers striding toward me. They're in the standard ZedSec uniforms—black, with black goggles and masks, and yellow stripes on each arm. They look sinister, like angry wasps.

"Identify," says the first one.

"McNab, Surep," I say.

He pauses. I know he's reading my details off his display.

"You were on the scene at the time of the fire," the officer says.

"I came to see Miriam—" I start to explain.

"You have smoke damage. You've been inside. Did you start this?"

"What? No! I went in to rescue her!" I protest.

He ignores me. "Was this a robbery attempt? Protection racket? Answer me!"

Am I imagining this? Did I breathe in fumes or something? ZedSec are always trouble, but this seems *weird.* Why would they think it was me? I wasn't even here first! I glance around, but the crowd has slipped away . . .

I take a step back.

"Halt!" snarls the officer. "Resisting Zephyr Security in its lawful duty is an offense. We are authorized to use force!"

"What?" I say.

"Do not resist!"

"I'm not resisting!" I shout, sticking my hands up.

The officer leans back as if I just tried to hit him. "Suspect is violent!" he says. "Apprehend!"

The other officer moves in from the side, swinging his stick. I duck and it swishes over my head. What's going on? Now the first officer swings at me, catching my shoulder with a sickening thud.

"Ow!" I yell.

I have to get out of here. I slam my skates together and leap backward. The hover motors throb as I race away. The officers chase after me.

“C’mere, you little runt!” shouts the first one, almost grabbing my jacket.

More officers are guarding the exit. Why are there so many? I peel off into the maze of

trash. Up ahead I can see the fence and a pile of old laptops leaning against it . . .

I jam my skates up to full, take two giant steps and leap to the top of the pile, then leap again. I grab the top of the fence and heave myself over. The skates squeal as they try to soften my landing, and I sprawl to the ground.

Down the street, someone's running toward me. On the other side of the fence, the officer is pulling out his gun. His *gun*! This can't be happening!

I don't stop to think. I drag myself up and skate into the night as fast as I can.

# 8

## Escape

I scramble across the wasteland beyond Miriam's warehouse.

"STOP!" shouts one of the ZedSec officers.

I don't stop. I jam my skates to full power, then leap and scramble over the next wall into a narrow alley. It's dark, but a spotlight shines down and I hear the buzzing blades of ZedSec drones above me.

"SUREP McNAB, YOU ARE UNDER ARREST!" calls a metallic voice. The lights slice back and forth around me. But they don't find me, and the officers are still clambering over the wall. *I can do this*, I think.

Then Sam says, “Urgent message from Zephyr Systems. Surep McNab, your actions have violated your warranty—”

“Not now, Sam!” I shout as I scramble over some old girders.

But Sam continues, “User ‘Surep McNab’ will be disabled unless you surrender. This is your only warning. Comply?”

“No! Of course I don’t comply!”

“User ‘Surep McNab’ disabled.”

My earpiece squeals, and my display goes black . . .

And I can’t breathe.

There’s no air coming into my mask. My cheeks suck inwards. I’m suffocating!

I stagger to a halt, grab at the mask, and tear it loose, gasping. Then I start coughing and can't stop. The Reek's poison and sulfur burn in my lungs. I collapse to my knees. The tank is screaming an error message. I can't breathe. I can't *breathe*.

No!

I drag my backpack open and pull out the new tank. Miriam's tank. My throat spasms. White spots appear in my vision like sparkling fog. I attach the tank with trembling fingers and switch it on . . .

The screaming stops. I hear a hiss, press the mask against my face and feel air flowing. I heave in a desperate breath. Then I cough again, but it's just the poison in my lungs from before. The air in the mask is pure, it's good. I can breathe. I'm alive . . .

My display is dead, my skates, too.

"Sam?" I say. No answer. I tap him. "Sam!"

Then a sound chimes, and Sam's voice says: "Rebooting . . . Welcome to Zephyr Systems. New user 'Sparrow' registered. Hello, Sparrow."

"What?" I gasp.

The display boots up, and suddenly I'm back online. The display shows everything working, even my old tank. But it's all under the user "Sparrow." How is that possible?

"Sam, what the *hell* is happening?" I say.

Sam's voice whispers in my ear, "Account 'Surep McNab' is invalid. I have created a new account for you on Zephyr Systems. You are no longer trackable."

I stare at the display. "HOW?" I demand.

"Miriam has upgraded me." Somehow, Sam's voice sounds like he's grinning.

I don't know what to think. It's like I've jacked into the middle of a game, and everyone else knows what's going on but me.

"Sam—" I say.

"ZedSec behind you, closing fast," he warns, and I realize I can hear sirens. The spotlights are still flashing across the alley, searching for me. I have to keep moving.

I'm near the docks and the river. The buildings are more spaced apart here, and the drones will see me if I try to run. I dart and weave and reach the narrow bridge, but there are lights up ahead, closing in, and more behind. ZedSec cars, which means I'm trapped.

"HALT!" shouts a voice ahead. "HALT OR WE WILL FIRE!"

I speed up. I'm at the middle of the bridge.

*Now.*

I fling out my tether, catch a lamppost, and leap forward. I feel the rope *twang* as it drags me around in a wide arc, 180 degrees right over the river. I lose height and land on the water—but my skates do their job, and I bounce off the surface and up again.

The world spins, and I hear someone screaming. I think it might be me. The bridge is looming up, and I judge the moment . . . *now*! I release the tether, skim over the bridge wall, and bounce onto the hood of the first ZedSec car and away.

I look down and see the ZedSec officers staring up at me, astonished. They should be looking at the road. I guess they forgot the cars coming the other way . . .

There is a *crash* behind me as the cars pile up on the bridge. *Yes!* That will take them a minute to sort out. But the drones are still above me. And there's a boat on the river with flashing blue lights. I've never seen so much security in my whole life.

I dash back along the waterfront. It's Saturday evening, and the pubs are full. There's a long outdoor restaurant, sealed by layers of protective plastic flaps. I slip inside and push past the crowd of patrons. Some of them move; some of them shove me away. One guy drops his drink and looks really angry.

“Sorry!” I shout.

The guy reaches out an arm to grab me, but I duck and he collides with a woman next to him. She turns, snarls, and hits him. Suddenly, there’s a brawl, and I’m in the middle, trying to crawl out. The fight spreads toward the river, and I follow it, staying under the punches. At the edge, I squeeze out under the flaps and then . . . There’s only one thing to do—I’m going into the water.

The shock of the cold grabs me and crushes my breath out in a *whoosh*. My display goes red again, and my skates drag me down. I have just enough time to switch to my old tank and check that it’s really working before I go under.

The water is dark and so cold that it moves like grease. And it’s filthy. But I force my eyes open and peer ahead. My mask is still tight around my face, and I clamp one hand over it.

"Warning," says Sam. "You appear to be underwater."

No kidding.

Will my skates work? I don't know. But they're too heavy to swim with. Gritting my teeth, I tap them together. There's a pulse, and I'm moving. My display shows so many warnings I can't even read them all. I ignore them and jet toward the ZedSec boat. I attach the tether magnet to the bottom and cling on.

Then I wait.

Sam whispers updates. The drones and officers are picking through the crowd on the shore. Someone is towing the cars off the bridge.

The boat moves away upstream, pulling me with it. It's so cold. I tuck my legs and arms in, shivering. Ten minutes is all I can manage, so I unhitch the tether and jet to the side as the boat moves on.

I find an old iron ladder and haul my way ashore. My arms feel like spaghetti. At last, I collapse on the side. I can't stop shaking.

I have to move. But where? I can't go home—Zephyr knows my address. *Miriam's*, I think. But that's it. I only have two safe places—home and Miriam's. And they're not safe anymore.

Who else can I trust? One of the other couriers? No. And anyway, they work for Zephyr. *Everyone* works for Zephyr.

There's only one other person.

I stagger to my feet. I'm soaking wet and freezing, and my muscles ache like I'm a hundred years old. I limp along the dark streets to a small neighborhood. Houses, not apartments. Even a small yard for each. I reach the house at the far end.

The lights are off. I head around the back and hide the new tank away in my bag. I hesitate. Then I scoop up some gravel stones and throw one at a window.

Nothing happens. I look around nervously and try again. There's a flicker of light, and the curtain moves.

Jamie's face stares down at me.

He doesn't look very friendly.

# 9

## Jamie

I wave up to Jamie at his window. He frowns.

Then he closes the curtains again.

*What?*

I stand there, stunned. What do I do now? He can't just ignore me like that!

Well . . . maybe he can, I realize. I remember our last conversation. I shouted at him for coming by my home, when the only reason he was there was to give Nina his old tablet. But so what? Jamie's so rich he can just give stuff away—how's that my fault? And now he's leaving me hanging when I actually *need* something! Something important, like saving my life, but he won't—

There's a click next to me, and the back door opens.

*Oh*, I think. *He just went to open the door. I knew that.*

The airlock whines softly, and Jamie steps outside.

"Let me in!" I mutter.

"Why?" he replies.

I don't know how to answer that. I can't stop shivering.

"Why are you all wet?" Jamie asks. "You been swimming or something?"

"Yeah."

Jamie blinks. He looks back into the house.

"Wait," he says.

Before I can answer, he goes back inside. When he returns, he's holding a huge old coat.

"Come on," he whispers.

"Jamie, you've got to help me," I mutter. "ZedSec are after me. They're—"

"Shh!" he snaps. "You'll wake Mom and Dad."

He leads me to a small shed, unlocks it, pushes me inside, then shuts the door behind us.

"What are you doing here, Surep?" he asks, his face hostile.

I swallow. "Listen, Jamie," I start. "I know I was a bit . . . uh, upset, before. But I'm in trouble. Big trouble. I need your help."

"What did you do?"

"Nothing! Look, please. I'm sorry about before. I said some stuff I shouldn't have."

"I worked for those exams," Jamie says in a hard voice. "The system's rigged, and it's unfair the way you've been treated. But that's not *my* fault."

"No, I know," I say. His voice starts to sound as if it's far away. This shed is nice. It's cozy. I'd like to sit down. Just for a moment. "I'm sorry. I just . . ."

"You're angry," Jamie says. "Don't you think I'm angry, too?"

"Absolutely," I agree. I nod to show him I agree. I don't know what he's talking about, but I bet if I sat down, I'd understand right away. Maybe I should sit down now. I nod again. I can't stop nodding. Nod, nod, nod.

"Surep?" Jamie asks. His voice swings back and forward like a ship at sea. "Surep, are you—"

Then the shed walls loom up around me, there's a blur and a faint clatter, and then nothing.

*

When I wake up, I'm in a weird wooden box surrounded by weapons, and a bear is lying on top of me.

I blink and look again.

Okay. The bear is really a huge heavy coat and a couple of blankets that smell musty. The weapons are garden tools, and the wooden box is a shed. I screw my eyes up and try to remember where I am.

Jamie. I'd been talking to Jamie, hadn't I? Then, with a groan, I remember the evening. Miriam, the fire, ZedSec going ballistic. A crazy chase across town, over the bridge. Someone saying, "YOU ARE UNDER ARREST." Am I? No, I realize. But I'm a . . . a *fugitive*.

And Miriam, hurt. “You have to deliver this to Axel Brodie!” she said. And the new tank. Oh, Lord, the new tank! I rifle through my bag, find it, and breathe a sigh of relief.

I sit up. Wow, I feel terrible.

I peer out of the shed window. It’s early evening—I must have slept all day. Then I hear a crunch outside, someone marching toward the shed. I gather myself up and tap my skates, ready to run . . .

The door opens, and Jamie looks at me.

“Hey,” he says.

I peer at him. “Hey.”

Jamie studies me with a rather strange expression. But all he says is, “Hungry?”

“Oh, wow, yes!” I reply.

He hands me a squashed roll, and I grab it. It's not easy eating with a mask. I have to lift it, take a bite, then lower the mask to chew. But I don't care, and I devour the roll in two bites.

"It's on the news," Jamie says. "About Miriam's place. She's in the hospital. They're saying you did it."

"I swear I didn't, Jamie. You've got to believe me—"

Jamie lifts a hand and says, "Come with me."

I frown. "Where?"

"Somewhere safe. That's what you want, right?" Jamie opens his backpack and pulls out a green hoodie. "Here. Hurry."

I watch him. There's something odd about him. I've known Jamie most of my life. We haven't spoken much lately, but I know when he's hiding something.

He's hiding something now.

I hesitate, but I don't have a choice. I have no other friends, no one who can help, no credits. "Where are we going?" I ask.

Jamie shrugs. "I told you. Somewhere safe."

"Right . . ." I pull the hoodie over my head and follow him.

Jamie leads me along tiny overgrown lanes between the houses, in the direction of the docks. We go down side streets, along passages, and past the backs of restaurants, where the air is hot and greasy and the ground is covered in old wrappers. These are forgotten places, without security cameras. I'm impressed—I'm a courier, but I've never been this way before. I didn't even know it existed.

Jamie stops and looks around. Then he grabs my sleeve and pulls me down a set of stone steps.

"Hey!" I protest, but he ignores me. He pushes me through a broken door and into a dark basement. "What's going on?"

"Here she is," Jamie says.

"What?" I screw up my eyes in the gloom. "Who's there? Jamie?"

A huge figure moves toward me out of the gloom. His neck is wide with muscle, his head is shaved, and his arms bulge under a tight white T-shirt. Beside him, a thin man leans forward, his hands in the pockets of his leather jacket. His face droops behind his mask.

They're the men I saw outside Miriam's place, watching it.

"Hello, dear," says the thin man, in a reedy voice. "Reckon you've got something of ours."

# 10

## Angels

Jamie is behind me, blocking my exit. The big man is blocking . . . well, everything.

I spin around and glare at Jamie. "What have you *done*?" I demand.

"He's helping us get back what's ours," says the thin man.

"I don't know what you're talking about," I say.

But Jamie coughs and says, "It's in her bag."

I scowl. The man holds out a hand. Maybe I could push past Jamie, get out before they came after me? But even as I think that, the big man steps forward, and the whole room darkens.

The floor seems to sink under his weight. The man's like a portable wall. There should be moss growing on him.

Jamie pulls the tank and Miriam's envelope from my bag and gives them to the thin man. He makes a face. "Dear me. Stealing from an old woman, huh?"

"I didn't *steal* it!" I snap. "Mir gave it to me!"

He looks at the envelope and asks, "What's this?"

"None of your business!" I say. "It's a delivery. You can't take it or tamper with it!" I'm too angry to be careful. "I saw you at her place. You started the fire!"

He shrugs. "Not us. Deliver to who?"

When I don't answer, the big man looms closer. He's really good at looming. He has to stoop or he'd bump his head on the ceiling, and I swear his arms are touching each wall. I swallow.

"To Axel Brodie," I finally reply.

"Hmm," says the thin man. Then, to my astonishment, he hands both items back to me. "She never mentioned an envelope."

I wonder whether I've been dreaming the last twenty-four hours, because nothing makes sense.

The thin man glances at the other man. "What do you think?" he asks.

The big man studies me for a long time. His eyes are pale gray and somehow familiar.

"Auntie likes her," he says at last, in a deep, clear voice.

"Wait," I say, staring at him. "Hang on. 'Auntie'? Auntie Miriam? Are you Lil' Billy?"

The big man blushes bright red, gives a little smile, and nods. The thin man shrugs. He seems to have made a decision.

"I'm Fergus," the thin man says. "We didn't burn down Miriam's place. When we arrived yesterday, ZedSec were already there."

"Yeah, because of the fire," I say.

"*Before* the fire," says Fergus. "They moved us on. Next thing we heard, Miriam's in the hospital and the warehouse is up in smoke." He points to the tank. "And that, too, so we thought."

Before the fire. ZedSec were there *before* the fire. But that means . . .

"They did it," says Jamie in a hard voice. "Zephyr burned down Miriam's place."

I look at him. "What's going on, Jamie?" I ask. "How do you know these guys?"

"Miriam had . . . an arrangement with us," says Fergus.

Lil' Billy nods. "We're business angels," he says seriously. "We provide"—he screws up his face and thinks—"*Financial Assistance and Security Services*. An' we got a van, too."

"Miriam said she could build something," says Fergus. "Something special. But it had to be unofficial. We fronted the cash, and Jamie here was the gofer."

"Gofer?" I ask, confused.

Fergus grins. "You know—'go for this,' 'go for that.' Gofer."

"Miriam needed someone to fetch equipment," explains Jamie. "Do some simple research. It had to be someone no one would suspect—not a real researcher, not a known face. Just . . . you know. A nerdy kid. The one who passes his exams, keeps his nose clean."

"But . . . *you*?" I say to Jamie. I can't believe it. "You're always the good one! Why would you even get involved?"

Jamie rolls his eyes. "Because of *you*!"

I stare at him, and he sighs.

"I mean, not just you," he says. "The system is broken, Surep. I go to school while you work twelve hours a day just to *breathe*. And Zephyr acts like they're gods!" He spits the words out angrily. "What did they do to your account when you ran?"

I think back and say, "They shut it down."

"They stopped your air. Zephyr can decide whether you're allowed to *breathe*. That's not right!"

"Your friend here reckons he can change the world," says Fergus. "Me and Billy, we're more like businessmen. Just looking for a bit of a return on our investment. Next thing we know, ZedSec has burned it all down." He shakes his head. "Tell me—does the tank work?"

I'm still trying to process Jamie's outburst, but at last I nod and say, "Yeah. I mean, I haven't tested it that much. But . . . yeah."

"You know *how* it works?" Fergus asks.

"No idea."

"Then, until Miriam wakes up, it's the only one in the world." Fergus points to the envelope. "Hey, maybe that's the plans?"

"They'd be digital," says Jamie. "You wouldn't put them in a letter."

"So what is it?" Fergus asks.

"Mir just said to deliver it," I say. "She did it properly—set up an in-person delivery request. Axel has to sign for it and everything."

That's not all she said. But I don't tell them that. I'm still not sure who I can trust.

Fergus examines me. "So, what are you going to do?" he asks.

I hold up the envelope. "Miriam ran back into the fire to get this," I say. "The delivery order was the last thing she did before she passed out. And I accepted the order." I shrug. "So I'm going to deliver it."

Zephyr Tower is the tallest building in Edinburgh and perhaps the most secure building in the world.

It stands in an old park south of the city center called the Meadows. It used to be a nice open area where folks could play soccer, picnic, or just hangout. Zephyr bought it, paved it over, and built a fortress. The tower is surrounded by massive walls, sixty feet high, with security guards and drones and surface-to-air weapon systems.

Inside, there's another wall. Inside *that*, there's a garden under a giant glass dome, full of trees and wildflowers—survivors of the Reek, kept alive by Zephyr. Then the tower itself—a thousand feet tall. A hundred floors.

Near the top, there's a dead zone where any active computer system will be detected.

And beyond that is Axel Brodie, whose security codes control the entire building.

It's impossible. There's no *way* I can deliver this letter. But to my surprise, Fergus, Lil' Billy, and Jamie look at each other and nod.

"Good," says Fergus with a grin. "We're in business. Time for Crawley."

# 11

## Crawley

"You'll need this," says Jamie, and shows me a computer chip the size of my fingernail. "Once you're inside, it will get you past some of the security."

"So how do I get inside?" I ask.

"Fergus is figuring that out," Jamie says. He smiles at my confusion. "Sorry, Surep. It wasn't supposed to go like this. Miriam wanted to bring you in properly. She had a plan, and we're part of it. *You're* part of it—perhaps the most important part. Did Miriam tell you *anything*?"

I remember her grabbing me and whispering in my ear with the last of her strength. Her words made no sense at the time, maybe still don't. But . . .

I nod and reply, "Yeah."

Jamie smiles again. It's a nice smile. I realize I've missed it. "Okay, then," he says, and holds out the chip. "May I?" He leans forward and plugs the chip into Sam, who chirrups.

Fergus turns back to us. "Crawley's ready," he says. "Let's go."

It's dark and deserted outside. Across the road is a battered green van, and Lil' Billy heaves himself into the driver's seat. The whole van leans to the side and creaks. We climb in the back, and Lil' Billy drives us to a shadowy space in the middle of town, behind an abandoned shopping center. Fergus leads us inside, past old signs, broken glass, and creepy frozen mannequins, then down to another basement. I remember again that new Edinburgh is built on top of old Edinburgh—there are layers and layers of history.

In the dark basement, someone is waiting. All I can see is his shadow and a faint glimmer of silver at his feet. Then he steps forward, and I realize the silver is the shine of his boots.

He grins at me and says, "Evening, Titch."

"*Bozo*?" I reply.

Bonzer's grin vanishes. "I *told* you—" he starts, but Fergus raises a hand.

"Evening, Bonzer," he says. "Is Crawley ready?"

Bonzer scowls but nods. "Yeah. This way."

He leads us to a rusted iron trapdoor in the floor and heaves it open. Then he clambers down an old metal ladder. Jamie follows.

Fergus nods to me and says, "Good luck, kid."

Lil' Billy gives me a hug that feels like a friendly building falling on me. He steps back, and I peer into the black hole.

Here goes.

I climb down ten feet or more before reaching the ground, and then I turn on Sam's flashlight. The ground is thick with mud, and the old brick walls are soaking wet. Water drips from the roof. I shiver.

Beyond us is a tunnel about as tall as me. It contains a huge, old rusted iron pipe covered in red mold and pale stalactites, with a narrow gap at the top.

"Here you go," says Bonzer. His voice echoes wetly, and his face gleams like a ghost in the beam from the flashlight.

"I don't understand," I say. "What *is* this?"

Bonzer grins. “Zephyr’s the future. Their stuff is all state of the art, world of tomorrow. But . . . they’re not too good on the past.” He taps the pipe, and it makes a dull *clang*. “This is Crawley Tunnel. They built it two hundred years ago to take water to the south side of

the city. Then they made new ones and forgot all about this. It even fell off the maps. But it's still intact."

Bonzer points down the tunnel. "It goes all the way from here to right under Zephyr Tower. A friend of mine works there. We, uh . . . move stuff from time to time. Zephyr's got no clue." He chuckles. "So, you going?"

I hesitate. But Jamie puts his hand on my shoulder, and I nod.

"Good," Bonzer says. "Follow the tunnel to the end. There's a service hatch. Easy." He steps back and examines his boots, now covered in mud. "Ick," he says.

Jamie goes ahead, holding his flashlight.

"Thanks," I say, suddenly, ". . . Bonzer."

He nods.

I follow Jamie.

*

Jamie and I crawl along the gap at the top of the pipe. The iron is slippery and cold beneath me, and my head brushes against the damp roof above. Wet blackness squeezes in around us. There are no rats left, thanks to the Reek, but cockroaches scurry away from us in waves, and my skin crawls.

After a while, we reach a kind of maintenance point for the pipe—a huge rusted wheel that I guess controlled the water flow once. Here we can stand up.

"Okay?" asks Jamie.

I almost laugh. Yesterday I was having a normal day, and now . . . "I can't believe *Bozo* is helping us," I say. "He hates me."

Jamie shakes his head. "It's not about you."

"Yeah, I guess. It's just, Bozo—"

“Who cares?” Jamie demands suddenly. “You and Bonzer, who cares? You and me, who cares?” His face looks fierce in the flashlight beam. “You know how Zephyr wins? They make us fight each other. You and Bonzer fighting about names. You hating me because I passed my exams. And all the time, Zephyr is laughing at us!”

I blink at him, shocked. “I don't . . . I don't hate you,” I say lamely.

Jamie waves a hand impatiently. “They used to call Edinburgh ‘Auld Reekie’—did you know that? Centuries ago. Back then, the reek was the smoke of the fires and the stink of the city. So the rich folks built new houses to get away. A whole New Town. They didn't want to fix things, you see? They just wanted them to happen only to poor people.”

Jamie scowls. “And nothing's changed!” he says. “The rich get richer and richer, crushing the rest until they have to work themselves to death for *air*. That's the real reek, Sparrow, the real poison! That's what matters—not some silly fight with Bonzer over a *nickname*!"

Jamie is almost panting with anger. Is this the bumbling boy who was my friend? I never knew he felt like this . . .

"I'm sorry," I say at last.

Jamie sighs. "Miriam says the only way to stop them is to reach Axel, and she's the smartest person I've ever met. So all of us—Fergus, Lil' Billy, Bonzer, me, *everyone*—are taking these risks so you can do that. Understand?"

I nod.

Jamie takes a breath. "Good," he says in a muffled voice. "Come on."

We carry on in silence. After another fifteen minutes, the tunnel ends in a pile of stones and broken bricks and a ladder. Above us is a hatch that looks surprisingly new.

“This is as far as I can go,” says Jamie. “That chip should get you past their systems. And I know Miriam upgraded Sam with some pretty cool new software. I don’t know what it’s for, but I trust her. You ready?”

I swallow. How could I possibly be ready? Yesterday all I cared about was new hover skates! But I hear Miriam’s desperate whisper. I see Jamie’s angry face.

“Y-yes,” I mutter.

Jamie hugs me. “Good luck. Sorry I shouted. I’m still your friend.”

I hug him back and say, “Me, too.”

I climb the ladder, disable Sam's flashlight, and lift the hatch carefully. Stale air whispers past me. I creep out.

I'm in a storage room.

I'm inside Zephyr headquarters.

# 12

## Delivery

The storage room is empty—just a few dusty filing boxes. I creep to the door and listen, then open it a crack and peer out. There's an airlock at the far end of the corridor. I go through, and I'm in a disused part of the main building.

It's quiet here, away from the offices and businesspeople. Sam puts a map up on my display, and I head for the service elevator. When we reach it, he says, "Processing—please wait."

I wait. The elevator arrives within a minute, though it feels like an hour. I step inside.

"Authentication required," says a voice from a glowing screen.

“Um . . . Sam?” I whisper.

“Please wait,” says Sam again.

“Authentication required,” repeats the voice. “Authentication— Thank you. Express route authorized.”

The doors close and the elevator rises, faster and faster. I grab the handrail as we shoot upward. Then the elevator slows so suddenly that my stomach flips. It stops, but the door doesn’t open. The screen goes dark.

I use my hover skates to help reach the ceiling, unclip the service hatch, and clamber up into the elevator shaft. Stenciled on the wall next to me is “Floor 90.” I close the hatch and start climbing the elevator cable. The skates help, but still, it’s hard work. A hot wind whistles past me in the shaft. If I fall now, it’s hundreds of feet down. Pancake time. I try not to think about it.

I climb.

At Floor 95, Sam beeps. “Electronic monitor zone,” he whispers. “I must shut down or I’ll be detected.”

I nod. My display goes dark, and my earpiece is silent. The world is darkness. My skates are dead.

I climb.

My heart thumps, and my arms burn. I can barely hold on. I glance down and wish I hadn't. The elevator shaft seems to go on forever.

Floor 97.

Floor 98. Something flutters near me in the dark. I let out a small scream and almost let go of the cable. My legs wrap around it as I desperately try not to fall, but I slip fifteen feet and shred my gloves. I hang, panting, waiting for my heart to stop doing somersaults. Then I climb again.

Floor 98.

Floor 99.

Floor 100.

I hold on with one hand and my knees so I can reach to my shoulder and reboot Sam. My screen lights up. I toss my tether gently toward the elevator wall, above an air shaft. It makes a huge *clang* as it lands just above the shaft, and I wince. But the magnet holds.

I hesitate for a moment. Then I swing back and launch forward, taking my weight on the tether. My arms scream in pain. I drag myself up, scramble into the air shaft, and collapse, panting.

"You have reached your destination," says Sam.

I wait in the darkness to catch my breath, then crawl forward. After a few yards, there's a panel. I open it, listen, then creep out.

I'm on the top floor of Zephyr Tower, in the hallway of Axel Brodie's home.

It's beautiful. There are gentle cream-colored walls and a rich striped carpet, nice plants, pieces of art. The air smells cleaner, fresher than I've ever smelled before.

Music plays quietly from the far room. I bring out Miriam's letter and unclip the tank. I take a deep breath and step into the room.

It's like the hall—gentle colors, nothing too bright. I thought there'd be more solid-gold doorknobs or something. One wall is bookshelves—real old books on real paper. One wall is a map of the world, with lines and comments scribbled all over it. There's a brass model of a machine on a table. I can make out the word "Babbage" engraved on the base, but I don't know what that means.

To one side is a large gray steel desk. It's not a pretty thing, just functional. Sitting at the desk, scribbling notes on a tablet, is Axel Brodie.

Axel is muttering as he writes, and he hasn't noticed me. Should I cough? Say "excuse me"? But then he leans back and stretches, removing his glasses and rubbing his eyes. He puts the glasses back on and stares at me.

“Um. Hello,” I say.

He doesn’t look alarmed. Instead, he gives an embarrassed smile. “I’m sorry,” he says. “I thought I knew all the cleaning staff . . .”

“I’m here to deliver something,” I say.

“Deliveries are downstairs at reception,” Axel says, looking confused. “But how did you get past—”

“To you personally,” I say. “From Miriam Fenn.”

Axel stops. “Miriam?” he says at last. “Wow.” He presses some buttons on his tablet and shuts it down. Then he stands, walks around his desk, and leans against it. “Okay, you’ve got my attention.”

“Miriam says you can stop this,” I say.

“Stop what?”

“Zephyr.”

Axel frowns. “I don’t understand—”

“We’re desperate out there!” I snap. I want to stay calm, but I can’t. “We’re working ourselves to death just to breathe! You don’t know what it’s like! Zephyr owns *everything*, and we have nothing left!”

Axel raises his hands, half to stop me, half in surrender.

“I understand,” he says softly. “Really, I do. But the Reek is everywhere, we’re no closer to finding a solution, and the purifier factories cost everything we have to run. If there was another way, I swear we’d do it. I’m just the head of tech here, but I promise we’re doing everything we can.”

Axel isn’t what I expected. He seems . . . sincere.

“I have a delivery for you,” I say, holding up the envelope. “You gotta sign.” I’m talking like he’s an ordinary customer. Like I haven’t broken into the home of the most powerful person in the world. I hold up the tank in my other hand. “And Miriam wanted you to see this.”

Axel glances at the letter, but it’s the tank that interests him. He’s a tech geek, after all. He examines it, and when he sees the fans underneath, he swallows.

“Is this what I think it is?” he asks.

I nod.

“And it . . . *works*?”

“Yes,” I reply.

“Oh, Miriam.” Axel whistles to himself and studies me. “Do you understand what this could mean?”

I smile. “Yeah. Miriam wanted you to have it—”

“FREEZE!”

I spin around. At the door are two ZedSec officers holding guns aimed at my head. More officers follow them, spreading out into the room and surrounding me.

“DROP YOUR WEAPON!” shouts the first one.

“I don’t have a weapon!” I yell.

“DROP IT!”

I drop the envelope and raise my hands.

“I surrender!” I squeak. “I’m not armed!”

One of the officers launches himself at me and slams me to the ground.

“Ow!” I yelp.

He drags my hands behind my back and cuffs them.

Axel hasn't moved. He gazes down at me.

Then he lifts the tank and smashes it against the steel table—once, twice, three times, until it is ruined—and throws the pieces aside.

# 13

## Values

"Pick her up," Axel says to the ZedSec officer. He's just destroyed the tank, the only working, portable, air-purifying tank *in the world*, but his voice is as calm and smooth as ever.

Axel smiles and says, "I liked Miriam, you know? She's almost as smart as me. But she has no head for business. All this . . ." He waves at the wrecked pieces. "What's the point? When Zephyr provides everything anyone needs?"

"But this tank could change the world!" I say.

"And what about the company?" Axel snaps. "Did you consider that? The economic damage this tank would do to Zephyr? The loss in sales, profits . . . *stock market value*? This would ruin us!"

"You're crazy." I stare at him. "This is crazy."

"This is *business*," Axel says. "This is the free market. Men like me deserve to gain from our investment. When the Reek came, *I* found a solution. I built the factories, the purifiers, the masks, the tanks, the infrastructure! And now you want to destroy it?"

"You did none of that!" I shout. "Other people built the factories and worked in them, and still work in them. And you pay them in *air*! It's not right!"

"It's how the world works, Surep," Axel says, shrugging. "Some people get rich, but the benefits trickle down to everyone—we lift the little people up with us, you see?"

"You're not lifting us—you're *crushing* us!" I stop. "Wait—how do you know my name?"

Axel smiles. “Oh, Surep. Did you honestly think I wouldn’t recognize you? We’ve been watching Miriam for months. All that hidden work, all that secret research . . . I knew she was up to something. I’ve known all along.”

I close my eyes. “*You* sent ZedSec to her place,” I mutter. “You ordered them to burn it down.”

“Very good!” Axel nods. “You know, you’re brighter than your exam scores suggest. You’ve got street smarts, I suppose, huh? Well. Be smart enough to know when you’re beaten. Miriam was a danger to our way of life, and I dealt with her. And if I have to, I’ll deal with you, too. And . . . Nina, is it? Your sister?”

A ball of cold fear settles in my stomach. Axel sees my expression and smiles again. He knows he’s won. The tank prototype is gone, Miriam is in hospital, and her place is in ruins. Axel was on to us the whole time.

My shoulders slump, and my legs almost give way. I'm so tired.

"I'm the world's smartest man, Surep," Axel says. "You never had a chance." He picks up the envelope. "And what's this? A begging letter? A threat?" He starts to open it.

"You gotta sign," I say weakly.

He glances at me.

"You gotta sign for it or I don't . . ." My head sinks. "Or I don't get paid."

"Ha!" Axel laughs. "Of course. Just here, is it?" He leans toward Sam and presents his face.

Sam beeps. "Authorized."

"There," Axel says, smirking. "I'll even leave you a tip."

“Sir, we should check the contents,” says an officer. Axel shrugs and hands the envelope over, and they scan it carefully. It takes them a few minutes, and Axel grins at me the whole time. I can barely lift my head to meet his gaze. The room is quiet. A light starts blinking on the phone on Axel’s desk, but he ignores it.

At last, the officer hands the envelope back, and Axel opens it. But then he frowns and says, “What’s this?”

The envelope is empty. There’s nothing at all.

“I don’t understand,” Axel says, looking confused.

His phone blinks again, and now there’s a commotion down the hallway. A woman is shouting at the ZedSec guys to let her in. Axel just stares at the envelope. “Why go to all this risk for nothing?” he says.

"Mr. Brodie!" the woman shouts. "Mr. Brodie, I have to speak to you! Axel!"

He looks up and nods to the officers, and the woman bursts into the room. She's wearing an expensive suit but looks like she's been running. Her hair is straggly around her red face.

"Mr. Brodie, something is *happening*!" she wails. "What are you doing?"

Axel stares at her blankly. "What?"

"You're sharing files!" she says. "Designs for a portable purifier? And company documents—*secret* documents! You have to stop!" The woman sees Axel's confused expression and flicks on the screen behind him.

Axel's face appears next to a news reporter.

"Secret Zephyr Company Files Released to Media," says the headline.

"Zephyr Hid Designs for Cheap Portable Purifier."

"Axel Brodie Issues Signed Confession—Admits Murder Attempt."

The newscaster looks appalled. A message ticker along the bottom shows Zephyr stock prices in red.

Axel takes it all in in a moment. "Fake," he says calmly. "It's fake news."

"But it's from your personal account, sir!"

Axel shakes his head. "Nonsense. No one can access my account without my authorization, and I certainly haven't—"

He stops.

He stares at me as I stand before him, grinning. He studies the envelope, then Sam, on my shoulder.

"What is that device exactly?" he asks faintly.

"Sam?" I reply with a shrug. "Just a smartpad. But Miriam upgraded him. He's really clever now. 'Street smarts,' you might say."

Axel's eye twitches. "A virus," he mutters. "You injected a virus into my account. This was all a *trick*. The letter, the tank, they weren't the point. You just needed me to sign. My personal authorization . . ."

Axel falls silent. Everyone stares at him.

"Look, everybody," I say. "It's the World's Smartest Man."

Axel turns to the woman. "Shut the broadcasters down," he demands. "Shut *everything* down!"

"We can't!" she wails. "Your account controls everything. We're locked out!"

Axel runs to his tablet and taps at it, but nothing happens. “I can’t access it!” he snaps. He slams his keyboard, tries again, but nothing works. My handcuffs fall to the floor as Sam deactivates them. More data spills up onto the screen. Axel sweeps his tablet off the desk.

“Stop this!” he roars. “Give me back control!”

“No,” I say.

“You can’t do this!” he shouts. “I’m Axel Brodie! You can’t *do* this!”

“It’s not nice feeling powerless, is it?” I ask. “It’s all going, Axel. We’re taking it back.”

Axel stops. He takes a single breath and looks around the room—at the guards and the woman and the screen. He swallows.

Then he leaps forward and wraps his hands around my throat.

We crash to the floor. I stare up into Axel's twisted furious face, his glasses askew. Behind him, the screen shows Sam's camera feed. The whole world is watching, and it's as if Axel's hands are around the throats of every person on Earth. The news reporter looks shocked, tapping her earpiece. The guards back away uncertainly.

“STOP IT!” Axel screams. “STOP IT NOW!”

His hands are tight. I can’t breathe. My world becomes gray around the edges. Slowly, painfully, I reach toward the belt. My fingertips stretch . . .

“GIVE IT TO ME!” Axel screams.

*Okay*, I think.

I press a button and my tether fires, smacks into Axel’s head, and knocks him out. He sprawls to the floor beside me.

“Mr. Brodie!” shouts the woman, rushing toward him. The guards lift their weapons.

“Sam, lights!” I croak.

The room goes dark. Someone screams, and there’s a sound of crashing. Sam shows an infrared overlay on my display so that I can stumble past the guards, down the hall to the main elevator. The doors close behind me, and the elevator descends.

At the bottom are ZedSec officers, staff, and employees carrying laptops and boxes of paper. They look frantic. Good. The screen here is replaying Axel's face as he tries to strangle me. People are watching in horror. Some of them are crying. Others are running out of the office into the gardens. The outer walls are still manned, but the gates are open. None of the security systems are working, and the guards can't receive orders.

I mingle with the office staff, hiding among them, and follow them out into the night as Zephyr Tower shuts down.

# 14

## Breathing

*Two weeks later.*

Miriam's awake. As soon as I enter the hospital ward, I can hear her voice barking orders, and when I reach her room, it's full of people. Most of them are in business suits. Some of them look worried, some excited.

"No one's suggesting we stop production," Miriam is saying. "But it doesn't need to be centralized. These designs allow local providers to set up their own workshops to build new units—"

A man in a suit keeps trying to interrupt, but Miriam glares at him until he stops. "*All* designs will be freely shared," she says in a voice like steel. “I don’t mind people making money, but they won’t profiteer from a worldwide medical emergency! Good grief, man, have some sense!”

“Hey,” I say.

Miriam looks up.

“You still owe me for those new skates,” she says.

I hold up a paper bag, and the smell of bhajis wafts into the room.

Miriam grins. “Everyone, get out.”

“But—” says Mr. Suit.

“OUT,” Miriam repeats.

They leave. Mr. Suit looks like he’s about to burst into tears. Miriam watches him with a kind but firm expression.

“There’s no profit angle,” she whispers to me. “It’s upsetting him. He doesn’t know what to do.”

“You’re feeling better, then,” I say.

Miriam tuts. “I’m perfectly fine. I keep telling the doctors to release me, but you know what they’re like.”

“Where will you go?” I ask. “The warehouse is gutted.”

“I might move into some office space,” she says. “There’s a place on the Meadows that isn’t being used anymore . . .”

I grin. We sit there for a bit, munching the bhajis.

“You were perfect,” Miriam says at last. “You completely fooled Brodie—he never imagined you could be a threat.” Then she shakes her head, and her voice drops. “But I didn't mean to put you at such risk. I'm sorry. I thought I'd have more time, but Brodie moved before I was ready. I didn't really expect you to . . . I mean, you could have . . ."

"It's okay," I say. "Really. It was just a delivery. That's my job, right? But . . . if you could leave me a review, that helps."

Miriam laughs.

"What happens now?" I ask. "Zephyr's bust, but people still need clean air. What are they going to do?"

"With the computer virus active, we have control of Axel's money," says Miriam. "We'll keep the purifier factories running until we can build portable units. And with everyone working on it, I expect someone will improve on my design. If we all work together, perhaps . . . perhaps we could even reverse things."

"Cure the Reek?" I ask. Saying it out loud seems ridiculous. It's been there my whole life.

But Miriam nods. "Cure the Reek."

"And Axel?" I say.

Miriam scowls. "He's on the run. But he's got nowhere to go. And the kind of friends he has don't last long when the money runs out . . ." She smiles. "We'll get him."

"So that's it, then," I say.

"Not quite." Miriam rummages around under her pillow for her smartpad and taps it against Sam.

"Transaction complete," says Sam.

Miriam nods. "Bit of a reward for you," she says, in an almost apologetic voice.

I check my balance. Then I check it again. Then I count the zeros and try to do the math in my head. When I look up, Miriam looks shifty.

"Axel doesn't know it, but he's been donating to lots of good causes recently," Miriam explains. "Including a new trust set up for promising youths who, for whatever reason, didn't pass their exams first time. Call this an investment. You can use it to go back to school. Or start a company. Or go on vacation, for all I care. Goodness knows you've earned it . . ."

"We could get a better place with this," I say. "And a new school uniform for Nina."

Miriam snorts. She's right, I realize. With this money, I could buy the *school*. What will I do?

Miriam yawns. I realize she's not as recovered as she pretends to be, and her face is gray. I stand up just as a nurse comes in to

check on her. The nurse frowns at the bhaji crumbs.

"Ms. Fenn has to rest now," he says, and I nod.

"Take care of yourself," I say, kissing her forehead.

Miriam smiles. "The trick is to take care of each other."

I leave.

Outside, it's a bright morning. It's been raining, but now it's sunny and the wet buildings sparkle under a pale blue Edinburgh sky. I check my tank—it's one of the new ones, first off the production line. Jamie, Fergus, and Lil' Billy have gone into business making them. The tank has a brand stamped on it—a flag with the words "Breathe Free." I fasten my mask and take a breath of clean air.

Then I kick my skates into life and head off to see what the day will bring.

Our books are tested
for children and young people by
children and young people.

Thanks to everyone who consulted on
a manuscript for their time and effort in
helping us to make our books better
for our readers.

# For more pulse-pounding adventures, check out:

Everyone Can Be a Reader

CHRIS BRADFORD
STELLAR
No air. No sound. No help in sight.

CHRIS BRADFORD
LUNAR
Mission Control, is anyone there?